JAMARI

Mary R. Toomey

VANTAGE PRESS
New York

Illustrated by Jeff Mayes

FIRST EDITION

Copyright © 1991 by Mary R. Toomey

Published by Vantage Press, Inc.
516 West 34th Street, New York, New York 10001

Manufactured in the United States of America
ISBN: 0-533-09132-2

1 2 3 4 5 6 7 8 9 0

To my nephew Jimmy who inspired me to write this book.

And to my dear husband, Bill, and my wonderful children, and my special friends who were so supportive of me—especially Larry M.

JAMARI

Way out in the universe, high in the sky, there is a planet called Orr. This is the home of Jamari. Jamari is a robot. He lives in a crater.

One summer's day Jamari exclaimed to his mother, "I'm very lonely. There is no one to play with me!" His mother suggested that he take a ride in his little spaceship.

So, Jamari took his mother's advice and went for a ride.

On that lonely day, Jamari wandered out into the universe in his little spaceship and landed on Earth.

Jamari parked his spaceship and started up a hill. Much to his surprise, he saw children playing in a schoolyard. He was a little frightened at what he saw.

Jamari hid behind a rock and peeked from behind it to get a better look. The children saw him and asked him to play with them.

When Jamari stepped from behind the rock, the children laughed because he was so cute. They became instant friends. *Someone just my size to play with*, thought Jamari. He was beginning to forget all about being lonely.

When Jamari saw the swing set in the schoolyard, he couldn't imagine how it was used. The children helped their little friend onto the swing.

"Push your feet," said the children, and Jamari was amazed when the swing started to move.

"Now to teach him how to play jump-rope," said the children. They gathered around Jamari, and two of the children took an end of the rope and started to swing. "Jump," said the children, so Jamari jumped.

When Jamari landed on the ground, he was surprised, because there is little gravity on his planet. His surprised look made the children giggle.

Would you believe that Jamari never played Dodge Ball? You are right, he never did. The children lined up to play.

When Jamari didn't run out of the way of the ball, it hit his antenna and bent it. All of the children were worried. They thought they had hurt him.

Just as they approached Jamari, his little antenna straightened itself up again. He smiled. The children were so pleased that he was not hurt.

The children said, "Let's give him a ride on the seesaw." After they seated him on the seesaw, one of the children sat on the other end. Jamari's end of the seesaw went up in the air.

Oh! How do I get down? thought Jamari.

Just then, the little girl on the other end pushed down with her feet, and her end went up and Jamari's came down. For the first time, the children heard Jamari make a sound. It sounded like a little giggle.

Suddenly the school bell rang. That was the end of recess. The children had to go back into school, and Jamari had to head back home.

As Jamari was leaving, the children all waved good-bye. He started down the hill to his little spaceship with joy in his heart. He thought, *I like it here, and I'm coming back.*

Jamari headed home after a very exciting day on Earth.

When the children were seated at their desks, their teachers asked if they had had a good time in the schoolyard. The children excitedly told how they had played with a cute little robot.

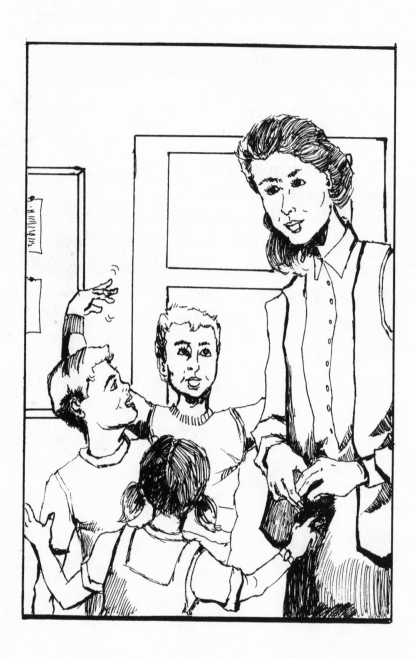

The teachers got together and delighted in the children's story about a little robot. "My, what an imagination children have!" they exclaimed.

Only Jamari and the children know
the truth.